from Archie

WRITTEN AND ILLUSTRATED BY VINCENT X. KIRSCH

to Zack

Abrams Books for Young Readers • New York

For everyone who will ever love

The illustrations in this book were made with watercolor, Black Star ink, and graphite and colored pencil on 140-lb. hot press watercolor paper.

Library of Congress Control Number 2019953707

ISBN 978-1-4197-4367-2

Text and illustrations copyright © 2020 Vincent X. Kirsch
Book design by Pamela Notarantonio

Printed and bound in China
10 9 8 7 6 5 4 3 2 1

Abrams Books for Young Readers are available at special discounts when purchased in quantity for premiums and promotions as well as fundraising or educational use. Special editions can also be created to specification. For details, contact specialsales@abramsbooks.com or the address below.

Abrams® is a registered trademark of Harry N. Abrams, Inc.

 ABRAMS The Art of Books
195 Broadway, New York, NY 10007
abramsbooks.com

"Archie loves Zack!"

"Zack loves Archie!"

Everyone said it was so.

Archie couldn't say it.

Zack couldn't say it.

But they wanted to.

At last, Archie
wrote to Zack.

From A. to Z.
It's true.
I love you.

Archie read his note
again and again.

It made him happy.

He didn't give it to Zack.

He hid the note.

Archie started over.

From A. to Z.
It's true.
I love you
very much.

Archie read his note
again and again.

It made him happy.

He didn't give it to Zack.

Something's still missing.

He hid the second note.

Archie wrote another.

From A. to Z.
It's perfectly
true.
I love you
very much.

Archie read his note
again and again.

It made him very happy.
It was exactly what he
wanted to say.

He almost gave it to Zack . . . but hid it instead.

Archie finally made up his mind
to give his note to Zack.

He looked for his last note.

It wasn't there.

He looked for the second note.

It wasn't there either.

Even the first note wasn't
where he hid it.

Zelda, Zinnia, and Zuzella knew who the notes were for.

Reading them made Zack
very happy.

Zack had a note he'd been

working on for a long time.

Zack read his note again and again.

Zack didn't give it to Archie.

Everyone knew it was so.